Viking Kong

WRITTEN BY TOMMY DONBAVAND
ILLUSTRATED BY LEO TRINIDAD

Franklin Watts
First published in Great Britain in 2016 by The Watts Publishing Group

Credits
Executive Editor: Adrian Cole
Design Manager: Peter Scoulding
Cover Designer: Cathryn Gilbert
Illustrator: Leo Trinidad

HB ISBN 978 1 4451 4673 7
PB ISBN 978 1 4451 4674 4
Library ebook ISBN 978 1 4451 4675 1

Printed in China

MIX
Paper from
responsible sources
FSC
www.fsc.org   FSC® C104740

Franklin Watts
An imprint of
Hachette Childr
Part of The Wat
Carmelite House
50 Victoria Emb
London EC4Y 0D

An Hachette UK
www.hachette.c

www.franklinwa

Contents

Chapter One:
Born

OK, so I wasn't exactly there when the big lad was born. Only a few select women from the village were allowed into the actual royal birthing chamber. But I was in the room next door with his father, King Harald. And, by all the gods, it was noisy!

Queen Ingrid was yelling and screaming — mainly about King Harald by the sound of it. The king was seated opposite me, squirming every time he heard his name mentioned, usually accompanied by some kind of rude insult.

Then there was the chanting of the village shaman — the only man given access to the birthing chamber. He was dancing around, casting spells, sprinkling herbs and spraying potions.

he royal nurse was adding to sounds. She was shouting at the shaman for getting in her way and, if I heard correctly, "making the birthing chamber smell like the inside of a pair of berserker's pants".

By contrast, the people assembled in our room remained utterly silent. Normally we'd have been chatting and gossiping like villagers on market day, but, while we were in the presence of the king, we had to be invited to speak. Which is why there was no chatter to cover up the increasingly nasty abuse coming through the wooden walls from the queen.

It was all rather awkward.

So, I was delighted when Arvid, one of the villagers charged with keeping the fires lit, entered through the side door. He dropped his latest delivery of logs next to the hearth and sat beside me, eyes fixed in the direction of the birthing chamber.

"Hi, Erik," he whispered. "How's it going in there?"

"How should I know?" I replied.

Arvid shrugged. "Your sister's in there, isn't she?"

"Yes," I said slowly. "Freya is in there, but I'm not."

"But, you're twins…"

I blinked. "That doesn't mean I can see through her eyes, Arvid. We're two different people!"

Arvid's thick eyebrows met in the middle of his face as he frowned and tried to work this one out. For a moment, he looked as though he was genuinely in pain from the effort of thinking. Then he sniffed and wiped his hands on his tunic.

"So, twins can't—"

"No!" I snapped. "Whatever it is you're about to suggest, we can't do it!"

I quickly stopped talking as the king shot a glance in my direction. He didn't look happy, which may have been because I was speaking, but it could also have been because Queen Ingrid had just shrieked that he was a *veslingr*, or "puny wretch", that was never allowed within sight of her again.

Then we heard the one sound we'd all been waiting for — the cry of a newborn baby.

We all jumped to our feet, clapping and cheering. The king stood, blushing above his beard and rubbing his hands together nervously.

"Go on, Sire!" I said. "Go and see."

As King Harald walked towards the queen's chamber, the door crashed open and my sister hurried out. "Oh, excuse me, Sire!" she said with a bow. She stepped aside as the king strode inside to meet his first-born child.

"Freya!" I called, catching her attention. My sister rushed across the room and flung her arms around me.

"It's a boy!" she exclaimed.

"Is he healthy?" I asked.

Freya's eyes sparkled in the way they do whenever she's bursting to tell me something. "You could say that!" she giggled.

We've never had a family of our own, Freya and I. We lost our parents when the village was attacked by a rival Viking clan known as Hellfire. We were just toddlers. The rest of the community had rallied round to bring us up, and now we'd been given the chance to pay the clan back by helping to look after the royal baby. It was a very proud day for us both.

And here he was! Carried out of the birthing chamber by his proud father — who was struggling under the weight of a child the size of a small bull!

"He's a big lad!" I gasped.

Freya giggled again. "The biggest I've ever seen!"

"This is a proud day for the Poowiff Clan!" proclaimed the king. "For, today, born unto us is your future leader, whom I shall name Prince Olf!"

Then both the king and huge prince crashed through the floor. Freya and I hurried over to help hold the new arrival.

Instantly, the shaman leapt out of the

chamber and began to dance around us, chanting spells and scattering herbs ... until the royal nurse finally lost her temper and knocked him out cold with a single blow of her meaty fist.

Chapter Two:
Birthday

"Happy birthday toooo yoouuuuu!"

The entire village cheered as Prince Olf sat in the water of the bay, playing with his present — a life-sized Viking longboat.

It was hard to believe that two years had gone by since the young prince had been born, and even harder to believe how much he'd grown in that time...

When he was three months old, Olf stood as tall as his father, and was already too big to be lifted up by one person on their own — and that included the largest and strongest of the clan's warriors. So the royal staff had been doubled to help the king and queen look after their pride and joy.

A special, reinforced cot had been built for Olf to sleep in, and teams of seamstresses worked around the clock to stitch both new clothing and nappies for the ballooning baby.

At six months old, the tribe's farmers had given up filling troughs with milk to feed the prince. Instead, they simply led cows up to his side, allowing him to pick them up and drink straight from the udder.

By the time Olf's first birthday came around, he was too large to fit inside any of the village huts, so lengths of material were stretched across the trees in a nearby wooded area, and both Freya and I began to live outdoors with the prince.

And the less said about the day last spring when we let him run around without a nappy on for a while — and the resulting wee-wee tsunami — the better.

Once we had heaved the birthday boy out of the water, the king and queen sat outside on their thrones and listened happily as Freya and I read Olf's greetings aloud.

"Greetings from the people of Tromsø!" I announced. "May Prince Olf continue to grow and be the pride of his clan!"

"And so he shall!" declared King Harald. "Although I won't mind so much if he doesn't listen to the 'keep growing' part."

"Best regards from Bergen," read Freya. "They have given Prince Olf the freedom of a city!"

Queen Ingrid frowned. "Don't you mean the freedom of *their* city?" she asked.

Freya examined the note again. "No, Your

Majesty," she said. "They've given him the freedom of Oslo instead. You may recall that, on the royal visit to Bergen earlier this year, your son sat on and destroyed their newly completed church..."

"Ah, yes," sighed the queen. "That poor, newly wed couple!"

"The greetings continue!" I cried. "This note comes all the way from..." I stopped and sniffed at the air. "Uh-oh," I said to my sister. "I think we may have a situation..."

I gave Freya a leg-up, and she climbed onto Olf's lap. "Phew!" she cried, pinching her nose. "Somebody needs changing!"

I pulled a horn from my belt and blew two sharp trills.

A moan went up around the village, but slowly everyone got to work. Teams of builders wheeled cranes into position, one of them led by Arvid.

"How much are we looking at?" he called over to me.

"Too early to say," I replied. "But he had three trees' worth of plums for breakfast this morning, so I'd be ready for anything!"

"Fair enough!" said Arvid. He turned to his team and gave the order: "Better get the big wheelbarrows!"

Carefully, Freya and I helped Olf to lie on his back — then one of his nurses climbed up and pulled out the old sword that served as a pin. Four others joined her to unfold the giant nappy, and everyone groaned again. This was a bad one!

"Heave!"

We looped ropes under Olf's arms, allowing the cranes to winch him up into the air — just enough for twenty gardeners

to scurry underneath and collect the
unpleasant contents of the nappy.

Not that anything would be going to waste
— all this stuff would be stored away and
used to fertilise crops in the future. The
clan already had enough fertiliser for the
next two hundred and eighty-five years.

Fully loaded barrows were wheeled away, allowing nurses with buckets and brooms to wash Olf. Finally, the old nappy was dragged down to the bay to be rinsed out. Then a replacement, made from stitched-together sails, was laid out underneath.

Olf was carefully lowered to the ground and the new nappy fastened. The large lad giggled as we helped him to sit up — just as his birthday cake was wheeled into view.

It was the size of a small lake with two burning trees in place of candles.

Prince Olf's face lit up at the sight of the treat. Taking a deep breath, he blew hard on the burning trees in front of him ... and set the entire village on fire.

Chapter Three:
Banished

It took three whole days and nights for the flames to be entirely extinguished. Afterwards, it was announced that the clan had lost over three quarters of its buildings, three longships and the forest had disappeared almost halfway to the Great Pine — a vast tree that towered even over Prince Olf himself.

The village elders and the king gathered

together in the smoking remains of the great hall for an urgent meeting. Leaving Freya to play peek-a-boo with Olf, I snuck in through a burned-down doorway to listen in from behind a fresh pile of timber.

"The child is dangerous!" claimed one elder, an ancient former warrior with a beard that hung down past his knees. "He put the entire village, and the whole population, at risk!"

"Perhaps," countered King Harald. "But he didn't know what he was doing..."

"Which makes it all the worse!" barked another elder, this one bald. "At least when we were raided by Hellfire all those years ago, we had the right to defend ourselves. But we can't unsheathe our swords against the threat of a giant baby!"

"We don't have to," said Arvid's grandfather. "We could hold a blót to honour the gods. Just imagine the good luck it could earn us."

"No!" roared the king, jumping up. "I will not allow you to sacrifice my son!"

"Then, what is the alternative?" demanded Long Beard. "Wait until he farts and blasts us all out into the middle of the ocean?"

"Prince Olf grows bigger by the day!" declared Fluffy Beard. "It is only a matter of time before he causes death on an unimaginable scale — whether he means to or not. The only course of action open to us is to banish him from the tribe."

I clamped my hand over my mouth to stifle my cry of dismay.

"We could do that," said Grandad Arvid, "or we could hold the biggest blót ever seen — people would come from miles around..."

"Silence!" bellowed the king. "I cannot believe you are threatening to banish my only son out of the protection of this clan and into the wilderness. I will not allow it!"

"It is not your decision," Fluffy Beard

reminded him. "All judgements decided by the elders are put to the vote."

"I vote for the blót. It's a sacrifice I'm prepared to make for a bit of peace..."

"Quiet, you!"

The king took his seat and sighed. "Very well," he said. "It appears I have little choice in the matter."

Baldy Beard smiled kindly. "It is for his own good as well as ours, Sire," he said. "We wish your son no harm. Now, let us vote..."

It was a close call. I remained hidden and watched as each of the elders put forward their point of view and chose whether to banish Olf or have him remain with the Poowiff Clan.

In the end, the numbers were tied —
seven votes for each side.

"Then, we are at an impasse," said Baldy
Beard.

"Perhaps not," said Fluffy Beard. "King
Harald has yet to cast his own vote.
Whichever course of action he chooses will
resolve the matter once and for all."

Slowly, the king stood, suddenly looking
older and more tired than I had ever seen
him. "This is the hardest decision I have
ever had to make," he said. "But I have
to think of my clan, and not just my own
flesh and blood." He took a deep breath.
"I vote to banish Prince Olf from the
Poowiff Clan."

Seconds later, I was racing back across the
smouldering village to where Olf and Freya
were waiting. Tears stung my eyes as I ran.
I couldn't believe the king had decided to
send his son out into the wilderness all
by himself.

I wasn't going to allow it! There was no way I would let Olf wander the forests and plains, scared and lonely. I had a plan.

It took me less than five minutes to explain everything to Freya. She was just as upset as I was, but agreed that there was only one course of action to take.

By the time the village elders arrived to make their announcement, Freya, Olf and I were long gone.

Chapter Four: Blame

At first, life in the wild wasn't particularly difficult — it was even a bit exciting. We had told Olf that we were going on a trip to celebrate his recent birthday, and the titanic toddler had plunged deep into the forest willingly.

Grabbing what few belongings we could carry, Freya and I followed.

We stopped for a while at The Great Pine. Olf had never seen a tree bigger than himself before, and he danced around it, feeling the rough bark beneath his fingers.

I took the opportunity to discuss our situation with Freya. "If the clan is going to follow us, this is as far as they will come," I explained.

"Really?"

I nodded. "The lands beyond the Great Pine are poorly charted, and home to

vicious creatures such as wolves and bears."

Freya shuddered. "Will we be safe there?"

"We have to be," I replied. "We can't go back."

"Home," said Olf quietly.

Freya and I looked up to find Olf staring back down the valley, over the tops of the trees to where smoke was still rising from the village on the edge of the bay.

"His first word!" my sister exclaimed.

"Home!" said Olf again, louder this time.

I reached up and patted his knee. "Maybe one day," I said. "But first, let's go on an adventure!"

And so the three of us turned our backs on the clan, and strode into the unknown lands ahead.

The next few weeks passed by quite quickly, although we had to make certain changes to Olf's daily routine. We couldn't winch him up to change his nappies, so we used our sewing kit (one of the things we'd been able to stuff into our pockets before fleeing the village) and turned his existing nappy into a pair of pants.

Of course, this meant we had to start potty training a huge toddler! Thankfully, Olf got the idea reasonably quickly, and we had very few accidents. Those we did have were cleaned away by swimming in sparkling rivers and under glistening waterfalls.

Food was plentiful at first — there was

still fruit on the trees as we headed into autumn. Freya proved herself to be an expert survivalist — teaching both Olf and me which plants we could eat, and which would make us ill.

We slept out in the open but, as the days began to shorten and the temperatures fell, we were forced to seek out caves for shelter at night. This wasn't easy, as we started to come across wild animals who also wanted the same accommodation. More than once, we were forced to scare away a pack of wolves or a grizzly bear with our fiery torches. By the third week of our "adventure", Freya and I began to take turns keeping watch while Olf slept.

By day, Freya set about teaching Olf to speak — something he took to very swiftly. He soon learned the names of the natural elements surrounding us. But his favourite word was still the one place he couldn't go: home.

"Where King Daddy?" he asked me one day while we were gathering wood for a fire. "King Daddy gone."

"Not exactly," I said. "King Daddy is in the village. We're the ones who are gone."

"Go home," said Olf. "Go King Daddy, Queen Mummy."

I sighed. This wasn't going to be simple to explain. "We can't," I said. "Not now. Not today."

"Home soon?"

I nodded and smiled. "Home soon," I said.

That night, Freya and I sat by the fire as Olf snored away, half in and half out of the only cave we'd been able to find.

"You told him we'd take him home?" Freya questioned.

"I didn't know what else to say," I admitted. "I couldn't tell him that 'King Daddy' wanted to get rid of him, could I?"

Freya pushed a piece of edible, if tasteless, plant root onto the end of a stick and held it in the crackling fire. "I suppose not," she sighed. "I just don't want to get his hopes up, that's all."

After we'd eaten the little amount of food we'd been able to find that day, I took first watch while my sister leaned back against Olf's leg and closed her eyes.

I sat in silence as the fire burned down, wondering just how I was going to tell Olf that ... we ... YAWN ... couldn't ... Zzzzzz...

Chapter Five: Battle

"Erik! Wake up! Olf is missing!"

I jerked awake, my eyes stinging as they faced the bright light of dawn. Oh no! I'd fallen asleep when I was supposed to be keeping watch.

"What?" I croaked. "How can Olf be missing? You can't lose someone that size!"

But it was true. The beast of a baby had disappeared. Thankfully, the path he had taken through the trees was easy to follow.

Pausing only to grab our belongings, Freya and I gave chase.

"He must have heard us talking last night," my sister said as we ran. "He's heading back to the village."

"How?" I demanded. "He doesn't know where it is."

"He can see over the treetops, remember? All he has to do is spot the Great Pine, and head for that."

It turned out that Freya was right. For almost the entire day we followed the trail of destruction that could only be made by a giant, lumbering toddler. Finally, we found Olf at the foot of the Great Pine.

And, he wasn't alone.

"King Harald!" I said. "What are you doing here?"

"Looking for you!" the king replied. "And I'm so happy I've finally found you."

"Olf not happy!" said the big baby. "Olf sad with King Daddy!"

King Harald gazed up at his son in wonder. "You can talk!" he exclaimed.

The youngster bent to glare at his father. "Where Queen Mummy?"

"Yes, well — that's the thing," said King Harald, his cheeks flushing red. "It turns out that Ingrid, your mother, was not at all happy that I voted to, er ... ask you to move out. That's why I'm out here searching. I have been every day for weeks now."

Then Olf did something I'd never seen him do before: he reached down and picked up his father. The king was like a doll in his hand.

"Aargh!" the clan leader shrieked. "What are you doing?"

"See Queen Mummy!" said Olf, and he began to climb the Great Pine.

Freya and I called for the prince to come down, but he wouldn't listen. Higher and higher he clambered, with his terrified father clutched in his grasp.

Olf stopped near the top of the tree. His weight caused the trunk to sway back and forth alarmingly.

"Bad men!" cried Olf, peering down the valley towards the village. "Bad men make Olf cross."

King Harald stopped his screaming long enough to follow his son's gaze. "By the gods, he's right!" he gasped. "It's Hellfire! The village is under attack again!"

Olf slid down the Great Pine. He stomped through the forest and burst out from the trees, roaring like something from the Underworld! King Harald was still clutched in the toddler's hand, while both Freya and I clung on to him for dear life.

The Viking warriors from the Hellfire clan turned and fled back towards their ships — but they were not fast enough. Olf dropped off his passengers and thundered after the Hellfire warriors, crashing through burning buildings and kicking aside carts.

He caught up with the screaming stragglers at the mudflats, stomping several of the intimidated invaders into the soft ground. Then he waded out to sea, heading straight for our enemy's longships.

Arrows, axes, swords and more were hurled at the advancing attacker — all of them bouncing off his skin without leaving a mark behind.

"Bad men go away!" he bellowed, lifting

a couple of ships out of the water and smashing them together. The occupants fell back into the sea, all thought of conquering the Poowiff Clan long forgotten. The Vikings of Hellfire wanted just one thing now: to escape with their lives.

Olf raised a foot and pushed another ship down under the surface, grinding its mighty wooden beams to little more than dust on the seabed. Then he snatched up a fourth ship, tipped it upside down to empty out the crew, placed it on his head and beamed back towards the shore.

"Olf a Viking now!" he giggled.

The celebrations went on long into the night. There was food, drink, dancing and lots and lots of laughter for Prince Olf as he tottered about, thoroughly enjoying himself. Freya and I sat with the king and queen. We were special guests at their table as a reward for looking after their son in the wilderness. We laughed as the big little guy tried to keep the longboat balanced on his head as he danced.

In fact, things would have been perfect had the village shaman not decided to perform his self-created ceremony of victory for us all. You could almost feel the atmosphere of joy melt away as he began to chant and hop from foot to foot.

It didn't last long, however. Olf had stuffed himself with good food after several weeks of eating nothing but plants and berries, and the banquet wasn't sitting too well in his tummy.

The shaman was only a few minutes into his performance when Olf leaned forwards and threw up all over him.

I reckon they could have heard our cheers on the other side of the ocean.

THE END

TOMMY DONBAVAND'S FUNNY SHORTS

They'll have you in stitches!

978 1 4451 4676 8

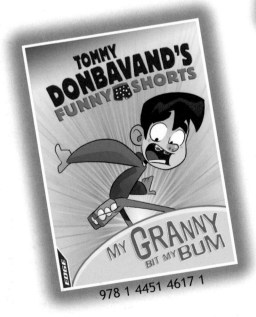

978 1 4451 4617 1

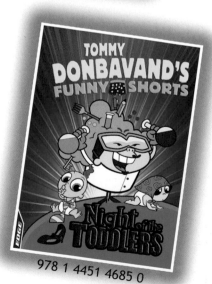

978 1 4451 4685 0

Contents

Introduction

Most people who have more than a passing interest in their health are aware nowadays of the problems associated with a diet that contains too much fat. A high level of fat consumption is linked to obesity, which in turn has been associated with coronary disease, diabetes and even cancer. The message that we should all cut down on our fat intake is reinforced every time we go shopping, and it is almost impossible to walk around a supermarket nowadays without noticing the huge variety of labels proclaiming foods that are low in fat or even fat-free.

Eating the low-fat way

Cutting the amount of fat in our diets is, of course, an effective way to lose weight, simply because it will reduce the number of calories we consume, as well as reducing the likelihood that we will contract a serious disease. However, before we cut fat out of our lives completely, it is important to remember that we all need to include a certain amount of fat in our daily intake of food if our bodies are to function properly. Essential fatty acids are needed to build cell membranes and for other vital body functions. Our brain tissue, nerve sheaths and bone marrow need fat, for example, and we all need fat to protect vital organs such as our liver, kidneys and heart.

Nutritionists suggest that we should aim to cut our intake of fat to 27-30 per cent of our total daily calorie intake. If your daily intake totals 2,000 calories, this will mean eating no more than about 75 g/2¾ oz of fat a day. Remember, however, that if you are pregnant or you are being treated for any medical condition, you must discuss with your doctor the changes you propose making in your diet before you begin your new regime. Also remember that a low-fat diet is unsuitable for children below the age of 5 years.

Fats can be broadly divided into two types: saturated and unsaturated. Saturated fats are those that are solid at room temperature, and they are found mainly in animal products – butter and cheese, high-fat meats (such as

sausages, pâté and bacon), and cakes, chocolate, potato crisps, biscuits, coconut, and hydrogenated vegetable oils or fish oils. Your should aim to reduce your intake of saturated fats to 8 per cent of your daily fat total, and consume the remainder in the form of unsaturated fats.

Unsaturated fats are healthier – but they are still fats. Unsaturated fats are usually liquid at room temperature and come from vegetable sources such as olive oil, groundnut oil, sunflower oil, safflower oil and corn oil. Remember, though, that oil is only another name for liquid fat. Using oil instead of margarine or butter to cook onions or garlic will do nothing to reduce your overall intake of fat.

Choosing low-fat ingredients

One of the simplest and most beneficial changes you can make in your diet is to change from full-fat milk, cream, cheese and yogurt to a low-fat or reduced-fat equivalent. Semi-skimmed milk, for example, has all the nutritional benefits of full-fat milk but only 2 per cent of milk fat compared with 3½ per cent in full-fat milk. Skimmed milk contains less than ½ per cent of milk fat. Use skimmed milk to make custards and sauces and you will not notice the difference in flavour. Also, low-fat yogurt or fromage frais mixed with chopped chives is a delicious and healthy alternative to butter or soured cream.

Most vegetables are naturally low in fat and can be used to make a meal of meat or fish go further. Most nutritionists recommend that we should all aim to eat

five portions of fresh fruit and vegetables every day because they contain antioxidant vitamins, including beta carotene (which creates vitamin A in the body) and vitamins C and E. Antioxidant vitamins in vegetables are thought to help prevent certain degenerative conditions (including cancer, heart disease, arthritis and ageing of the skin) and to protect the body from the harmful effects of pollution and ultraviolet light. Also, phytochemicals, which occur naturally in plants, are thought to be instrumental in the fight against cancer.

Key fat-reducing techniques

Steaming is the best way to cook vegetables to preserve their goodness. Boiling can destroy up to three-quarters of the vitamin C present in green vegetables. If you have to boil, cook the vegetables as quickly as possible and avoid overcooking, which also destroys the carotene.

If you have time, it is a good idea to make your own stock to use as the basis of casseroles and soups. Ready-made stocks and stock cubes are often high in salt and artificial flavourings. Instead, add fresh herbs and spices to the water you have used to cook vegetables or soak dried mushrooms. Liquids in which meat and fish of various kinds have been cooked can also be saved for stock. Chill the liquid in the refrigerator and you will easily be able to remove and discard the fat, which will have risen to the top of the container and solidified.

Pastas, noodles, pulses and grains can all be used in a low-fat diet, and they are useful for bulking out dishes. Pasta is available in a wide range of shapes and patterns, and is excellent for boosting your carbohydrate intake (inadequate intake of carbohydrate can result in fatigue and poor energy levels). Wholewheat pasta is particularly high in fibre, which helps speed the passage of waste material through the digestive system. Before you buy, check that noodles and pastas have not been enriched with egg. Choose wholewheat or rice varieties instead.

You can also stir cooked brown rice into soups and casseroles to thicken them, or mix one part red lentils with three parts lean minced beef to make a small amount of meat go further.

Equipment

Money spent on good-quality, non-stick saucepans and cookware will not be wasted. Not only will they directly reduce the amount of fat needed for cooking, they will save you time because they are easier to clean. Remember to use plastic implements or wooden spoons with non-stick pans so that you do not scratch the surfaces.

A ridged grill pan makes it possible to cook with the minimum amount of fat or oil because the fat drips down between the ridges rather than being absorbed by the food. Non-stick woks are also useful for stir-fries, or you can use a large, non-stick frying pan instead. When stir-frying, use the smallest possible amount of oil. Keep the heat constant and the food moving to ensure quick, even cooking.

Use a slotted spoon to remove food from the pan, so that cooking juices are left behind. Absorbent kitchen paper is useful for draining surface oil and fat from food that has just been cooked, but it can also be used to soak up fat that rises to the top of a pan during cooking. Use plain, unpatterned kitchen paper so that no dye is transferred to the food.

KEY	
Simplicity level 1–3 (1 easiest, 3 slightly harder)	
Preparation time	
Cooking time	

Spicy Lentil Soup

For a warming, satisfying meal on a cold day, this lentil dish is packed full of flavour and goodness.

NUTRITIONAL INFORMATION

Calories	155	Sugars 4g
Protein	. . . . .11g	Fat 3g
Carbohydrate	. . .22g	Saturates 0.4g

🥘 1 hr   🕐 1¼ hrs

SERVES 4

I N G R E D I E N T S

115 g/4 oz red lentils

2 tsp vegetable oil

1 large onion, finely chopped

2 garlic cloves, crushed

1 tsp ground cumin

1 tsp ground coriander

1 tsp garam masala

2 tbsp tomato purée

1 litre/1¾ pints vegetable stock

350 g/12 oz canned sweetcorn, drained

salt and pepper

TO SERVE

low-fat natural yogurt

fresh parsley, chopped

warmed pitta bread

1 Rinse the red lentils thoroughly under cold running water. Drain well and set aside.

2 Heat the oil in a large, non-stick saucepan and cook the onion and garlic gently until softened but not browned.

3 Stir in the cumin, coriander, garam masala, tomato purée and about 4 tablespoons of the stock. Mix well and simmer gently for 2 minutes.

4 Add the lentils and pour in the remaining stock. Bring to the boil, lower the heat, cover and simmer for 1 hour until the lentils are tender and the soup thickened. Stir in the sweetcorn and heat through for 5 minutes. Season to taste with salt and pepper.

5 Ladle into warmed soup bowls and top each with a spoonful of yogurt and a sprinkling of parsley. Serve with warmed pitta bread.

COOK'S TIP

Many of the ready-prepared ethnic breads available today either contain fat or are brushed with oil before baking. Always check the ingredients list for fat content.

Cucumber & Tomato Soup

Although this chilled soup is not an authentic Indian dish, it is wonderful served as a 'cooler' between hot, spicy courses.

NUTRITIONAL INFORMATION

Calories 73	Sugar 16g
Protein 2g	Fats 1g
Carbohydrates . . .16g	Saturates 0.2g

 12 hrs   0 mins

SERVES 6

INGREDIENTS

4 tomatoes, skinned and deseeded

1.5 kg/3 lb 5 oz watermelon, seedless if available

10-cm/4-inch piece of cucumber, peeled and deseeded

2 spring onions, green parts only, chopped

1 tbsp chopped fresh mint

salt and pepper

sprigs of fresh mint, to garnish

1 Using a sharp knife, dice 1 tomato into 1-cm/½ inch cubes.

2 Remove the rind from the watermelon and discard it, and remove the seeds if it is not seedless.

3 Put the 3 remaining tomatoes into a blender or food processor and, with the motor running, add the cucumber, spring onions and watermelon. Process until smooth.

4 If not using a food processor, push the deseeded melon and remaining tomatoes through a sieve into a bowl. Chop the cucumber and spring onions and then add them to the bowl with the melon and the tomatoes.

5 Stir the diced tomatoes and chopped mint into the melon purée, then adjust the seasoning to taste. Cover and chill the cucumber and tomato soup overnight in the refrigerator. Check the seasoning and transfer to a serving bowl. Garnish with mint sprigs.

COOK'S TIP
Although this soup does improve if chilled overnight, it is also delicious as a quick starter if whipped up just before a meal and served immediately.

Vegetable Soup with Bulgar

This healthy and colourful soup makes good use of your herb garden. The fresh herbs give it a vibrant flavour.

NUTRITIONAL INFORMATION

Calories	93	Sugars	. . . . .8g
Protein	. . . . .5g	Fat	. . . . .3g
Carbohydrate	. . .13g	Saturates	. . . . . . .0g

 10 mins   1 hr

SERVES 5–6

I N G R E D I E N T S

1 tbsp olive oil

2 onions, chopped

3 garlic cloves, finely chopped or crushed

55 g/2 oz bulgar wheat

5 tomatoes, skinned and sliced, or 400 g/ 14 oz canned plum tomatoes in juice

225 g/8 oz peeled diced pumpkin or acorn squash

1 large courgette, cut into quarters lengthways and sliced

1 litre/1¾ pints boiling water

2 tbsp tomato purée

¼ tsp chilli purée

40 g/1½ oz chopped mixed fresh oregano, basil and flat-leaved parsley

25 g/1 oz rocket leaves, roughly chopped

175 g/6 oz shelled fresh or frozen peas

salt and pepper

freshly grated Parmesan cheese, to serve

1 Heat the oil in a large saucepan over a medium-low heat and add the onions and garlic. Cook for 5–8 minutes, stirring occasionally, until the onions soften.

2 Stir in the bulgar and continue cooking, stirring constantly, for 1 minute.

3 Layer the tomatoes, pumpkin or squash, and courgette in the pan.

4 Combine half the boiling water with the tomato purée, chilli purée and a pinch of salt. Pour over the vegetables. Cover and simmer for 15 minutes.

5 Uncover the pan and stir. Put all the herbs and the rocket on top of the soup and layer the peas over them. Pour in the remaining water and gradually bring to the boil. Lower the heat and simmer for 20–25 minutes or until all the vegetables are tender.

6 Stir the soup. Taste and adjust the seasoning, adding salt and pepper, if necessary, and a little more chilli purée if you wish. Ladle into warmed bowls and serve with Parmesan cheese.

Mixed Bean Pâté

This is a really quick starter to prepare if canned beans are used. Choose a wide variety of beans for colour and flavour.

NUTRITIONAL INFORMATION

Calories 126   Sugars 3g
Protein ....5g   Fat 6g
Carbohydrate ...13g   Saturates 1g

45 mins   0 mins

SERVES 4

I N G R E D I E N T S

400 g/14 oz canned mixed beans, drained

2 tbsp olive oil

juice of 1 lemon

2 garlic cloves, crushed

1 tbsp chopped fresh coriander

2 spring onions, chopped

salt and pepper

shredded spring onions, to garnish

1 Rinse the beans thoroughly under cold running water and drain well.

2 Transfer the beans to a food processor or blender and process until smooth. Alternatively, place the beans in a bowl and mash thoroughly by hand with a fork or potato masher.

3 Add the olive oil, lemon juice, garlic, coriander and spring onions and blend until fairly smooth. Season with salt and pepper to taste.

4 Transfer the pâté to a serving bowl, cover and chill in the refrigerator for at least 30 minutes.

5 Garnish the pâté with shredded spring onions and serve.

Carrot & Potato Soufflé

Hot soufflés have a reputation for being difficult to make, but this one is both simple and impressive. Make sure you serve it as soon as it is ready.

NUTRITIONAL INFORMATION

Calories	294	Sugars	.........6g
Protein	........10g	Fat	...........9g
Carbohydrate	...46g	Saturates	.......4g

🥧 15 mins 🕐 40 mins

SERVES 4

INGREDIENTS

2 tbsp butter, melted

4 tbsp fresh wholewheat breadcrumbs

3 floury potatoes, baked in their skins

2 carrots, grated

2 eggs, separated

2 tbsp orange juice

¼ tsp grated nutmeg

salt and pepper

carrot curls, to garnish

1 Brush the inside of an 850-ml/1½-pint soufflé dish with the butter. Sprinkle about three-quarters of the breadcrumbs over the bottom and sides.

2 Cut the baked potatoes in half and scoop the flesh into a mixing bowl.

3 Add the carrots, egg yolks, orange juice and nutmeg to the potato flesh. Season to taste with salt and pepper.

4 In a separate bowl, whisk the egg whites until soft peaks form, then gently fold into the potato mixture with a metal spoon until well incorporated.

5 Gently spoon the potato and carrot mixture into the prepared soufflé dish. Sprinkle the remaining breadcrumbs over the top of the mixture.

6 Cook in a preheated oven, 200°C/ 400°F/Gas Mark 6, for 40 minutes until risen and golden. Do not open the oven door during the cooking time, otherwise the soufflé will sink. Serve immediately, garnished with carrot curls.

COOK'S TIP

To bake the potatoes, prick the skins and cook in a preheated oven, 190°C/375°F/ Gas Mark 5, for about 1 hour.

Capri Salad

This tomato, olive and mozzarella salad, dressed with balsamic vinegar and extra-virgin olive oil, makes a delicious starter on its own.

NUTRITIONAL INFORMATION

Calories	95	Sugars	........3g
Protein	.........3g	Fat	..........8g
Carbohydrate	....3g	Saturates	.......3g

20 mins   3–5 mins

SERVES 4

INGREDIENTS

2 beef tomatoes

125 g/4½ oz mozzarella cheese

12 black olives

8 fresh basil leaves

1 tbsp balsamic vinegar

1 tbsp extra-virgin olive oil

salt and pepper

fresh basil leaves, to garnish

1 Using a sharp knife, cut the tomatoes into thin slices.

2 Drain the mozzarella, if necessary, and cut into slices.

3 Stone the black olives and slice them into rings.

4 Layer the tomatoes, mozzarella, olives and basil leaves alternately in a stack, finishing with a layer of cheese on top.

5 Place each stack under a preheated hot grill for 2–3 minutes or just long enough to melt the mozzarella.

6 Drizzle over the balsamic vinegar and olive oil, and season to taste with a little salt and pepper.

7 Transfer to individual serving plates and garnish with fresh basil leaves. Serve immediately.

COOK'S TIP

Buffalo mozzarella cheese, although it is usually more expensive because of the comparative rarity of buffalo, does have a better flavour than the cow's milk variety. It is popular in salads, but also provides a tangy layer in baked dishes.

Mango Salad

This is an unusual combination but works well as long as the mango is very unripe. Papaya can be used instead, if you prefer.

NUTRITIONAL INFORMATION

Calories 26	Sugars 3g	
Protein 1g	Fat 0.2g	
Carbohydrate 6g	Saturates 0g	

🎩 10 mins   🕐 0 mins

SERVES 4

I N G R E D I E N T S

1 large, unripe mango, peeled and cut into long, thin shreds

1 small fresh red chilli, deseeded and finely chopped

2 shallots, finely chopped

2 tbsp lemon juice

1 tbsp light soy sauce

6 roasted canned chestnuts, cut into quarters

1 watermelon, to serve

1 lollo biondo lettuce, or any crunchy lettuce

15 g/½ oz coriander leaves

1 Soak the mango briefly in cold water to remove any syrup. Meanwhile, combine the chilli, shallots, lemon juice and soy sauce. Drain the mango and combine with the chestnuts.

2 To make the melon basket, stand the watermelon on one end on a level work surface. Holding a knife level and in one place, turn the watermelon on its axis so that the knife marks an even line all around the middle. Mark a 2.5-cm/1-inch-wide handle across the top and through the central stem, joining the middle line at either end. (If you prefer a zigzag finish, mark the shape to be cut at this point

before any cuts are made, to ensure an even zigzag line.)

3 Take a sharp knife and, following the marks made for the handle, make the first vertical cut. Then cut down the other side of the handle. Now follow the middle line and make your straight or zigzag cut, taking care that the knife is always pointing towards the centre of the watermelon

and is level with the work surface. This ensures that, when you reach the handle cuts, the cut-out piece of melon will pull away cleanly.

4 Hollow out the flesh with a spoon, leaving a clean edge. Line the melon basket with the lettuce and coriander. Fill with the salad, pour over the dressing and serve immediately.

Mixed Bean & Apple Salad

Use any mixture of beans you have to hand in this recipe,
but the wider the variety, the more colourful the salad.

NUTRITIONAL INFORMATION

Calories 183	Sugars 8g
Protein 6g	Fat 7g
Carbohydrate . . .26g	Saturates 1g

20 mins   20 mins

SERVES 4

I N G R E D I E N T S

225 g/8 oz new potatoes, scrubbed and cut
  into quarters

225 g/8 oz mixed canned beans, such as
  red kidney beans, small cannellini beans
  and borlotti beans, drained and rinsed

1 red eating apple, diced and tossed in
  1 tbsp lemon juice

1 yellow pepper, deseeded and diced

1 shallot, sliced

½ fennel bulb, sliced

oakleaf lettuce leaves

D R E S S I N G

1 tbsp red wine vinegar

2 tbsp olive oil

1½ tsp mild yellow mustard

1 garlic clove, crushed

2 tsp chopped fresh thyme

1 Cook the potatoes in a saucepan of boiling water for 15 minutes until tender. Drain and transfer to a large bowl.

2 Add the mixed beans to the potatoes, along with the diced apple and yellow pepper, and the sliced shallot and fennel. Mix thoroughly, taking care not to break up the cooked potatoes.

3 To make the dressing, whisk all the dressing ingredients together until thoroughly combined, then pour it over the potato salad.

4 Line a serving plate or salad bowl with the oakleaf lettuce leaves and spoon the potato mixture into the centre. Serve the salad immediately.

VARIATION

Use Dijon or whole-grain mustard in place of mild yellow mustard for a different flavour.

Prawn & Noodle Salad

This delicious combination of rice noodles and prawns, lightly dressed with typical Thai flavours, makes an impressive starter or light lunch.

NUTRITIONAL INFORMATION

Calories	204	Sugars	........8g
Protein	........15g	Fat	...........3g
Carbohydrate	...29g	Saturates	.......1g

 15 mins   2 mins

SERVES 4

I N G R E D I E N T S

85 g/3 oz rice vermicelli or rice sticks

175 g/6 oz mangetouts, cut crossways in half, if large

5 tbsp lime juice

4 tbsp Thai fish sauce

1 tbsp sugar

2.5-cm/1-inch piece of fresh root ginger, finely chopped

1 fresh red chilli, deseeded and thinly sliced diagonally

4 tbsp chopped fresh coriander or mint, plus extra to garnish

10-cm/4-inch piece of cucumber, peeled, deseeded and diced

2 spring onions, thinly sliced diagonally

16–20 large cooked prawns, peeled

2 tbsp chopped unsalted peanuts or cashew nuts (optional)

TO GARNISH

4 whole cooked prawns

4 lemon slices

1 Put the rice noodles in a large bowl and pour over enough hot water to cover. Set aside for about 4 minutes until soft. Drain and rinse under cold running water; drain again and set aside.

2 Bring a saucepan of water to the boil. Add the mangetouts and return to the boil. Lower the heat and simmer for 1 minute. Drain the mangetouts, rinse under cold running water until cold, then drain and set aside.

3 Whisk together the lime juice, fish sauce, sugar, ginger, chilli and coriander or mint in a large bowl. Stir in the cucumber and spring onions. Add the drained noodles, mangetouts and the prawns. Toss the salad together gently.

4 Divide the noodle salad among 4 large plates. Sprinkle with chopped coriander or mint, and the peanuts, if using. Garnish each plate with a whole prawn and a lemon slice. Serve immediately.

Warm Tuna Salad

This colourful, refreshing starter is perfect for a special occasion. The dressing can be made in advance and spooned over just before serving.

NUTRITIONAL INFORMATION

Calories 127	Sugars 4g	
Protein 13g	Fat 5g	
Carbohydrate 6g	Saturates 1g	

 15 mins   8 mins

SERVES 4

I N G R E D I E N T S

55 g/2 oz Chinese leaves, shredded

3 tbsp rice wine

2 tbsp Thai fish sauce

1 tbsp finely shredded fresh root ginger

1 garlic clove, finely chopped

½ small fresh red bird-eye chilli, finely chopped

2 tsp soft light brown sugar

2 tbsp lime juice

400 g/14 oz fresh tuna steak

sunflower oil, for brushing

125 g/4½ oz cherry tomatoes

chopped fresh mint leaves and fresh mint sprigs, to garnish

1 Place a small pile of shredded Chinese leaves on a serving plate. Place the rice wine, fish sauce, ginger, garlic, chilli, brown sugar and 1 tablespoon of the lime juice in a screw-top jar and shake well to combine evenly.

2 Cut the tuna into strips of an even thickness. Sprinkle with the remaining lime juice.

3 Brush a wide frying pan or ridged grill pan with the oil and heat until very hot. Arrange the tuna strips in the pan and cook until just firm and lightly golden, turning them over once. Remove and set aside.

4 Add the tomatoes to the pan and cook over a high heat until lightly browned. Arrange the tuna and tomatoes over the Chinese leaves and spoon over the dressing. Garnish with chopped fresh mint and sprigs of mint and serve warm.

COOK'S TIP

You can make a quick version of this dish using canned tuna. Just drain and flake the tuna, omit steps 2 and 3 and continue as in the recipe.

Lobster Risotto

This is a special occasion dish, just for two. However, you could easily double the recipe for a dinner party if necessary.

NUTRITIONAL INFORMATION

Calories ....487 Sugars 8g
Protein ....10g Fat 10g
Carbohydrate ...86g Saturates 2g

15 mins   35 mins

SERVES 2

INGREDIENTS

1 cooked lobster, about 400–450 g/ 14 oz–1 lb

4 tbsp butter

1 tbsp olive oil

1 onion, finely chopped

1 garlic clove, finely chopped

1 tsp fresh thyme leaves

175 g/6 oz arborio rice

600 ml/1 pint simmering fish stock

150 ml/5 fl oz sparkling wine

1 tsp green or pink peppercorns in brine, drained and roughly chopped

1 tbsp chopped fresh parsley

1 To prepare the lobster, remove the claws by twisting. Crack the claws using the back of a large knife and set aside. Split the body lengthways. Remove and discard the intestinal vein, the stomach sac and the spongy gills. Remove the meat from the tail and roughly chop. Set aside with the claws.

2 Heat half the butter and all the oil in a large frying pan. Add the onion and cook gently for 4–5 minutes until softened. Add the garlic and cook for another 30 seconds. Add the thyme and rice. Cook, stirring, for 1–2 minutes until the rice is well coated and translucent.

3 Increase the heat under the pan to medium and begin adding the stock, a ladleful at a time, stirring well between additions. Continue for 20–25 minutes until all the stock has been absorbed.

4 Add the lobster meat and claws. Stir in the wine, increasing the heat. When the wine is absorbed, remove the pan from the heat and stir in the peppercorns, remaining butter and parsley. Set aside for 1 minute, then serve immediately.

VARIATION

For a slightly cheaper version, substitute 450 g/1 lb prawns for the lobster.

Barbecued Clams

Cook with Mexican flair by serving clams from
the barbecue, topped with a spicy sweetcorn salsa.

NUTRITIONAL INFORMATION

Calories	189	Sugars 9g
Protein	........23g	Fat 2g
Carbohydrate	...21g	Saturates 1g

🕐 35 mins   ⏱ 10 mins

SERVES 4

I N G R E D I E N T S

2 kg/4 lb 8 oz live clams

5 ripe tomatoes

2 garlic cloves, finely chopped

225 g/8 oz canned sweetcorn, drained

3 tbsp finely chopped fresh coriander

3 spring onions, thinly sliced

¼ tsp ground cumin

juice of ½ lime

½–1 fresh green chilli, deseeded and
   finely chopped

salt

lime wedges, to serve

1 Place the clams in a large bowl. Cover with cold water and add a handful of salt. Set aside to soak for 30 minutes.

2 Meanwhile, skin the tomatoes. Place them in a heatproof bowl, pour boiling water over to cover and leave to stand for 30 seconds. Drain and plunge into cold water. The skins will then slide off easily. Cut the tomatoes in half, deseed then chop the flesh.

3 To make the salsa, combine the tomatoes, chopped garlic, sweetcorn, coriander, spring onions, cumin, lime juice and chilli in a bowl. Season with salt to taste. Cover and set aside.

4 Drain the clams, discarding any that remain open. Cook the clams over the hot coals of a barbecue, allowing about 5 minutes per side. They will pop open when they are ready. Discard any that remain closed.

5 Transfer to a plate. Top with the salsa, and serve with lime wedges for squeezing over the clams.

VARIATION
Mussels can be
used very successfully
in place of the clams.

Curry Crust Cod

An easy, economical main dish that transforms a plain piece
of fish into an exotic meal – try it with other white fish too.

NUTRITIONAL INFORMATION

Calories ....223 Sugars 1g
Protein ....31g Fat 4g
Carbohydrate ...16g Saturates 0g

 15 mins   35–40 mins

SERVES 4

I N G R E D I E N T S

½ tsp sesame oil

4 cod fillets, about 150 g/5½ oz each

85 g/3 oz fresh white breadcrumbs

2 tbsp blanched almonds, chopped

2 tsp Thai green curry paste

rind of ½ lime, finely grated

salt and pepper

lime slices and rind, and mixed salad
    leaves, to garnish

boiled new potatoes, to serve

COOK'S TIP

To test whether the
fish is cooked through, use a
fork to pierce it in the thickest part –
if the flesh is white all the way
through and flakes apart
easily, it is cooked sufficiently.

1 Brush the sesame oil over the bottom
of a wide, shallow casserole or
roasting tin, then arrange the pieces of
cod in it in a single layer.

2 Combine the fresh breadcrumbs,
chopped almonds, curry paste and
grated lime rind in a bowl, stirring well to
blend thoroughly and evenly. Season to
taste with salt and pepper.

3 Spoon the crumb mixture over the
fish, pressing down lightly. Bake in a
preheated oven, 200°C/400°F/Gas Mark 6,
for about 35–40 minutes until the fish is
cooked through and the curry crumb
topping is golden brown.

4 Serve hot, garnished with lime slices,
lime rind and mixed salad leaves, and
accompanied by boiled new potatoes.

Steamed Stuffed Snapper

Red mullet may be used instead of the snapper, although their size makes them a little more difficult to stuff. Use one mullet per person.

NUTRITIONAL INFORMATION

Calories 406   Sugar 4g
Protein . . . . .68g   Fat 9g
Carbohydrate . . . .9g   Saturates 0g

🧊 20 mins   🕐 10 mins

SERVES 4

I N G R E D I E N T S

1.3 kg/3 lb whole snapper, cleaned and scaled

175 g/6 oz spinach

orange slices and shredded spring onions, to garnish

S T U F F I N G

55 g/2 oz cooked long-grain rice

1 tsp grated fresh root ginger

2 spring onions, finely chopped

2 tsp light soy sauce

1 tsp sesame oil

½ tsp ground star anise

1 orange, segmented and chopped

1 Rinse the fish inside and out under cold running water and pat dry with kitchen paper.

2 Blanch the spinach for 40 seconds, rinse in cold water and drain well, pressing out as much moisture as possible.

3 Arrange the spinach on a heatproof plate and place the fish on top.

4 To make the stuffing, combine the cooked rice, grated ginger, spring onions, soy sauce, sesame oil, star anise and orange in a bowl.

5 Spoon the stuffing into the body cavity of the fish, pressing it in well with a spoon.

6 Cover the plate and cook in a steamer for 10 minutes or until the fish is cooked through.

7 Garnish the fish with orange slices and shredded spring onions and serve.

COOK'S TIP

The name 'snapper' covers a family of tropical and subtropical fish that vary in colour. They may be red, orange, pink, grey or blue-green and almost all have a fine flavour. They range in size from 15 cm/6 inches to 90 cm/3 feet.

Braised Fish Fillets

Almost any white fish, such as lemon sole or plaice, can be used to make this delicious dish with a Chinese flavour.

NUTRITIONAL INFORMATION

Calories . . . . .107 Sugars 2g
Protein . . . . .17g Fat 2g
Carbohydrate . . . .6g Saturates 0.3g

🍴 35 mins   🕙 10 mins

SERVES 4

I N G R E D I E N T S

3–4 small Chinese dried mushrooms

280–350 g/10–12 oz fish fillets

1 tsp salt

½ egg white, lightly beaten

1 tsp cornflour

600 ml/1 pint vegetable oil

1 tsp finely chopped fresh root ginger

2 spring onions, finely chopped

1 garlic clove, finely chopped

½ small green pepper, deseeded
    and diced

½ small carrot, thinly sliced

55 g/2 oz canned sliced bamboo shoots,
    drained and rinsed

½ tsp sugar

1 tbsp light soy sauce

1 tsp rice wine or dry sherry

1 tbsp chilli bean sauce

2–3 tbsp vegetable stock or water

a few drops of sesame oil

1 Soak the dried mushrooms in a bowl of warm water for 30 minutes. Drain thoroughly on kitchen paper, reserving the soaking water for stock or soup. Squeeze the mushrooms to extract all of the moisture, cut off and discard any hard stalks and slice the caps thinly.

2 Cut the fish into bite-sized pieces, then place in a shallow dish and mix with a pinch of salt, the egg white and the cornflour, turning the fish to coat well.

3 Heat the oil in a preheated wok. Add the fish pieces to the wok and deep-fry for about 1 minute. Remove the fish pieces with a slotted spoon and drain on kitchen paper.

4 Carefully pour off the excess oil, leaving about 1 tablespoon in the wok. Add the ginger, spring onions and garlic and cook over a medium heat for a few seconds to flavour the oil, then add the green pepper, carrot and bamboo shoots and stir-fry for about 1 minute.

5 Add the sugar, soy sauce, rice wine or sherry, chilli bean sauce, stock or water, and the remaining salt and bring to the boil. Add the fish pieces, stirring to coat with the sauce, and cook for 1 minute. Sprinkle with a few drops of sesame oil and serve.

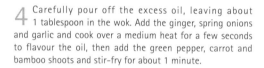

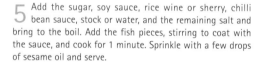

Rice Noodles with Chicken

The great thing about stir-fries is you can cook with very little fat and still get lots of flavour, as in this light, healthy lunch dish.

NUTRITIONAL INFORMATION	
Calories 329	Sugars 3g
Protein 25g	Fat 4g
Carbohydrate . . .46g	Saturates 1g

25 mins   10 mins

SERVES 4

INGREDIENTS

200 g/7 oz rice stick noodles

1 tbsp sunflower oil

1 garlic clove, finely chopped

2-cm/¾-inch piece of fresh root ginger, finely chopped

4 spring onions, chopped

1 fresh red bird-eye chilli, deseeded and sliced

300 g/10½ oz skinless boneless chicken, finely chopped

2 chicken livers, finely chopped

1 celery stick, thinly sliced

1 carrot, cut into fine batons

300 g/10½ oz shredded Chinese leaves

4 tbsp lime juice

2 tbsp Thai fish sauce

1 tbsp soy sauce

2 tbsp shredded fresh mint

slices of pickled garlic

sprig of fresh mint, to garnish

1 Soak the rice noodles in hot water for 15 minutes or according to the packet instructions. Drain well.

2 Heat the oil in a wok or large frying pan and stir-fry the garlic, ginger, spring onions and chilli for 1 minute. Stir in the chicken and chicken livers, then stir-fry over a high heat for 2–3 minutes until beginning to brown.

3 Add the celery and carrot and stir-fry for 2 minutes to soften. Add the Chinese leaves, then stir in the lime juice, fish sauce and soy sauce.

4 Add the noodles and stir to heat thoroughly. Sprinkle with shredded mint and pickled garlic. Serve immediately, garnished with a mint sprig.

Sweet Maple Chicken

You can use any chicken portions for this recipe. Thighs are economical for large barbecue parties, but you could also use wings or drumsticks.

NUTRITIONAL INFORMATION

Calories ....122 Sugars 16g
Protein ....11g Fat 1g
Carbohydrate ...17g Saturates 1g

   35 mins   20 mins

SERVES 6

INGREDIENTS

12 boneless chicken thighs

5 tbsp maple syrup

1 tbsp caster sugar

grated rind and juice of ½ orange

2 tbsp ketchup

2 tsp Worcestershire sauce

TO GARNISH
orange slices

sprigs of fresh parsley

TO SERVE
Italian bread, such as focaccia

salad leaves

cherry tomatoes, cut into quarters

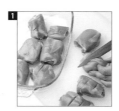  

1 Using a long sharp knife, make 2–3 diagonal slashes in the flesh of the chicken to allow the flavours to permeate. Arrange the chicken thighs in a single layer in a shallow, non-metallic dish.

2 To make the marinade, combine the maple syrup, sugar, orange rind and juice, ketchup and Worcestershire sauce in a small bowl.

3 Pour the marinade over the chicken, turning the chicken well to coat thoroughly. Cover with clingfilm and chill in the refrigerator until required.

4 Remove the chicken from the marinade, reserving the marinade.

5 Transfer the chicken to the barbecue and cook over hot coals for 20 minutes, turning the chicken and basting with the marinade frequently. Alternatively, cook under a preheated grill for 20 minutes, turning and basting.

6 Transfer the chicken to warmed serving plates and garnish with slices of orange and sprigs of parsley. Serve immediately with Italian bread, fresh salad leaves and cherry tomatoes.

Glazed Turkey Steaks

Prepare these steaks the day before they are needed and serve in toasted ciabatta bread, accompanied by crisp salad leaves.

NUTRITIONAL INFORMATION

Calories	219	Sugars	.........4g
Protein	........28g	Fat	..........10g
Carbohydrate	....4g	Saturates	......1g

🍤 12 hrs   🕐 15 mins

SERVES 4

I N G R E D I E N T S

100 g/3½ oz redcurrant jelly

2 tbsp lime juice

3 tbsp olive oil

2 tbsp dry white wine

¼ tsp ground ginger

pinch of grated nutmeg

4 turkey breast steaks

salt and pepper

TO SERVE

mixed salad leaves

vinaigrette dressing

1 ciabatta loaf

cherry tomatoes

1 Place the redcurrant jelly and lime juice in a pan and heat gently until the jelly melts. Add the oil, wine, ginger and nutmeg.

2 Place the turkey steaks in a shallow, non-metallic dish and season with salt and pepper. Pour over the marinade, turning the meat so that it is well coated. Cover and chill overnight.

3 Remove the turkey from the marinade, reserving the marinade for basting, and grill on an oiled rack over hot coals for about 4 minutes on each side. Baste the turkey steaks frequently with the reserved marinade.

4 Meanwhile, toss the salad leaves in the vinaigrette dressing. Cut the ciabatta loaf in half lengthways and place, cut side down, at the side of the barbecue. Cook until golden. Place each steak on top of salad leaves, sandwich between 2 pieces of bread and serve immediately with cherry tomatoes.

COOK'S TIP

Turkey and chicken scallops are also ideal for cooking on the barbecue. Since they are thin, they will cook through without burning on the outside. Leave them overnight in a marinade of your choice then cook, basting with a little lemon juice and oil.

Turkey & Vegetable Loaf

This impressive-looking turkey loaf is flavoured with herbs and a layer of juicy tomatoes and covered with courgette ribbons.

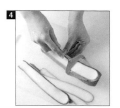

NUTRITIONAL INFORMATION

Calories 165	Sugars 1g	
Protein 36g	Fat 2g	
Carbohydrate 1g	Saturates 0.5g	

 10 mins   1¼ hrs

SERVES 4

I N G R E D I E N T S

1 onion, finely chopped

1 garlic clove, crushed

900 g/2 lb lean minced turkey

1 tbsp chopped fresh parsley

1 tbsp chopped fresh chives

1 tbsp chopped fresh tarragon

1 egg white, lightly beaten

2 courgettes (1 medium, 1 large)

2 tomatoes

salt and pepper

tomato and herb sauce, to serve (optional)

1 Line a non-stick loaf tin with baking paper. Place the onion, garlic and turkey in a bowl, add the herbs and season to taste with salt and pepper. Mix with your hands, then add the egg white to bind together.

2 Press half of the turkey mixture into the bottom of the tin. Trim and thinly slice the medium courgette and the tomatoes and arrange the slices over the meat. Top with the rest of the turkey mixture and press down firmly.

3 Cover with a layer of kitchen foil and place in a roasting tin. Pour in enough boiling water to come halfway up the sides of the loaf tin. Bake in a preheated oven, 190°C/375°F/Gas Mark 5, for about 1–1¼ hours, removing the foil for the last 20 minutes of cooking. Test that the loaf is cooked by inserting a cocktail stick into the centre – the juices should run clear. The loaf will also shrink away from the sides of the tin.

4 Meanwhile, trim the ends from the large courgette. Using a vegetable peeler or hand-held metal cheese slice, cut the courgette lengthways into thin slices. Bring a pan of water to the boil and then blanch the courgette ribbons for 1–2 minutes until just tender. Drain and and keep them warm.

5 Remove the turkey loaf from the tin and transfer to a warm serving platter. Drape the courgette ribbons over it. Serve the loaf with a tomato and herb sauce, if desired.

Duck with Berry Sauce

Duck is a rich meat and is best accompanied by piquant fruit, as in this sophisticated dinner party dish.

NUTRITIONAL INFORMATION

Calories	293	Sugars	........10g
Protein	........28g	Fat	...........8g
Carbohydrate	...13g	Saturates	......2g

1¼ hrs   30 mins

SERVES 4

INGREDIENTS

450 g/1 lb boneless duck breasts

2 tbsp raspberry vinegar

2 tbsp brandy

1 tbsp honey

1 tsp sunflower oil, for brushing

salt and pepper

SAUCE

225 g/8 oz raspberries, thawed if frozen

300 ml/10 fl oz rosé wine

2 tsp cornflour blended with 4 tsp cold water

TO SERVE

2 kiwi fruit, peeled and thinly sliced

assorted vegetables

  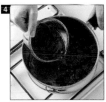

1 Skin and trim the duck breasts to remove any excess fat. Using a sharp knife, score the flesh in diagonal lines and pound it with a meat mallet or a covered rolling pin until it is 1.5 cm/⅝ inch thick.

2 Place the duck breasts in a shallow dish. Combine the vinegar, brandy and honey in a small bowl and spoon it over the duck. Cover and chill in the refrigerator for about 1 hour.

3 Drain the duck breasts, reserving the marinade, and place on a grill rack.

Season and brush with a little oil. Cook for 10 minutes under a preheated grill, turn over, season and brush with oil again. Cook for another 8–10 minutes until the meat is cooked through.

4 Meanwhile, make the sauce. Reserve about 55 g/2 oz raspberries and place the rest in a pan. Add the reserved marinade and the wine. Bring to the boil and simmer for 5 minutes until slightly reduced. Strain

the sauce through a fine sieve, pressing the raspberries through with the back of a spoon. Return the liquid to the pan and add the cornflour paste. Heat through, stirring, until thickened. Add the reserved raspberries and season to taste.

5 Thinly slice the duck breasts and alternate with slices of kiwi fruit on warm serving plates. Spoon over the sauce and serve with a selection of vegetables.

Steak in a Wine Marinade

Fillet, sirloin, rump and entrecôte are all suitable cuts
for this dish, although rump steak retains the most flavour.

NUTRITIONAL INFORMATION	
Calories 356	Sugars 2g
Protein 41g	Fat 9g
Carbohydrate 2g	Saturates 4g

🔥 3 hrs   🕐 15 mins

SERVES 4

INGREDIENTS

4 rump steaks, about 250 g/9 oz each

600 ml/1 pint red wine

1 onion, cut into quarters

2 tbsp Dijon mustard

2 garlic cloves, crushed

4 large field mushrooms

olive oil, for brushing

branch of fresh rosemary (optional)

salt and pepper

1 Snip through the fat strip on the steaks in 3 places, so that the steak retains its shape when cooked.

2 Combine the red wine, onion, mustard, garlic and salt and pepper in a bowl. Lay the steaks in a shallow, non-porous dish and pour over the marinade. Cover and chill in the refrigerator for 2–3 hours.

3 Remove the steaks from the refrigerator 30 minutes before you intend to cook them to allow them to come to room temperature. This is specially important if the steak is thick, so that it cooks more evenly and is not well done on the outside and raw in the middle.

4 Seal both sides of the steak – about 1 minute on each side – over a hot barbecue. If the steak is about 2.5 cm/ 1 inch thick, keep it over a hot barbecue and cook for about 4 minutes on each side. This will give a medium-rare steak – cook it more or less, to suit your taste. If the steak is a thicker cut, move it to a less hot part of the barbecue or further away from the coals. To test the readiness of the meat while cooking, simply press it with your finger – the more the meat yields, the less it is cooked.

5 Brush the mushrooms with the olive oil and cook them alongside the steak for 5 minutes, turning once. When you put the mushrooms on the barbecue, put the rosemary branch, if using, in the fire to flavour the meat slightly.

6 Remove the steak and set aside to rest for 1–2 minutes before serving. Slice the mushrooms and then serve immediately with the meat.

Sweet & Sour Venison Stir-fry

Venison is super-lean and low in fat, so it's the perfect choice for a
healthy diet. Cooked quickly with crisp vegetables, it's ideal in a stir-fry.

NUTRITIONAL INFORMATION

Calories	219	Sugars	........18g
Protein	........23g	Fat	..........5g
Carbohydrate	...20g	Saturates	.......1g

🍚 15 mins   🕐 15 mins

SERVES 4

I N G R E D I E N T S

1 bunch of spring onions

1 red pepper

100 g/3½ oz mangetouts

100 g/3½ oz baby corn cobs

350 g/12 oz lean venison steak

1 tbsp vegetable oil

1 garlic clove, crushed

2.5-cm/1-inch piece fresh root ginger,
  finely chopped

3 tbsp light soy sauce, plus extra for serving

1 tbsp white wine vinegar

2 tbsp dry sherry

2 tsp honey

225 g/8 oz canned pineapple pieces in
  natural juice, drained

25 g/1 oz beansprouts

freshly cooked rice, to serve

1 Cut the spring onions into 2.5-cm/
1-inch pieces. Halve and deseed the
red pepper and cut it into 2.5-cm/1-inch
pieces. Trim the mangetouts and baby
corn cobs.

2 Trim any fat from the meat and cut it
into thin strips. Heat the oil in a large
frying pan or wok until hot and stir-fry the
meat, garlic and ginger for 5 minutes.

3 Add the spring onions, red pepper,
mangetouts and baby corn cobs, then
stir in the soy sauce, vinegar, sherry and
honey. Stir-fry for another 5 minutes.

4 Carefully stir in the pineapple pieces
and beansprouts and cook for another
1–2 minutes to heat through. Serve with
freshly cooked rice and extra soy sauce
for dipping.

VARIATION
For a nutritious meal-in-one,
cook 225 g/8 oz egg noodles in
boiling water for 3–4 minutes. Drain
and add to the pan in step 4, with the
pineapple and beansprouts. Add an
extra 2 tablespoons soy sauce with
the pineapple and beansprouts.

Gnocchi with Tomato Sauce

Freshly made potato gnocchi are delicious, especially when they are topped with a fragrant tomato sauce.

NUTRITIONAL INFORMATION

Calories . . . . .216 Sugars 5g
Protein . . . . .5g Fat 6g
Carbohydrate . . .39g Saturates 1g

30 mins   45 mins

SERVES 4

I N G R E D I E N T S

350 g/12 oz floury potatoes, halved

85 g/3 oz self-raising flour, sifted, plus extra for dusting

2 tsp dried oregano

2 tbsp vegetable oil

1 large onion, chopped

2 garlic cloves, chopped

400 g/14 oz canned chopped tomatoes

½ vegetable stock cube dissolved in 100 ml/3½ fl oz boiling water

2 tbsp fresh basil, shredded, plus whole leaves to garnish

salt and pepper

Parmesan cheese, freshly grated, to serve

1 Bring a large saucepan of water to the boil. Add the potatoes and cook for 12–15 minutes or until tender. Drain and set aside to cool.

VARIATION

The gnocchi can also be served with a pesto sauce made from fresh basil leaves, pine kernels, garlic, olive oil and pecorino or Parmesan cheese.

2 Peel the potatoes and then mash them with the salt and pepper, sifted flour and oregano. Mix together with your hands to form a dough.

3 Heat the oil in a frying pan. Add the onions and garlic and cook for about 3–4 minutes. Add the tomatoes and stock and cook, uncovered, for 10 minutes. Season with salt and pepper to taste.

4 Roll the potato dough into a sausage about 2.5 cm/1 inch in diameter. Cut the sausage into 2.5-cm/1-inch lengths. Flour your hands, then press a fork into each piece to create a series of ridges on one side and the indent of your index finger on the other side.

5 Bring a large saucepan of water to the boil, add the gnocchi, in batches, and cook for 2–3 minutes. They should rise to the surface when cooked. Remove from the pan with a slotted spoon, drain well and keep warm while you are cooking the remaining batches.

6 Stir the basil into the tomato sauce and pour over the gnocchi. Garnish with basil leaves and season with pepper to taste. Sprinkle with grated Parmesan and serve immediately.

Savoury Flan

This tasty flan combines a delicious filling of lentils and red peppers in a crisp wholemeal crust.

NUTRITIONAL INFORMATION

Calories	287	Sugars	.........5g
Protein	........10g	Fat	...........5g
Carbohydrate	...35g	Saturates	.......3g

45 mins 50 mins

SERVES 8

I N G R E D I E N T S

PASTRY

225 g/8 oz plain wholemeal flour

100 g/3½ oz margarine, cut into small pieces

4 tbsp water

FILLING

175 g/6 oz red lentils, rinsed

300 ml/10 fl oz vegetable stock

1 tbsp margarine

1 onion, chopped

2 red peppers, deseeded and diced

1 tsp yeast extract

1 tbsp tomato purée

3 tbsp chopped fresh parsley

pepper

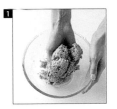  

1 To make the pastry, place the flour in a mixing bowl and rub in the margarine. Stir in the water and bring together to form a dough. Wrap and chill in the refrigerator for 30 minutes.

2 Meanwhile, make the filling. Put the lentils in a saucepan with the stock, bring to the boil and simmer for 10 minutes until tender. Mash to a purée.

3 Melt the margarine in a small pan and cook the onion and peppers, stirring frequently, until just soft. Stir in the lentil purée, yeast extract, tomato purée and parsley. Season with pepper.

4 On a lightly floured work surface, roll out the dough and line a 24-cm/9½-inch loose-based quiche tin. Prick the bottom with a fork and spoon the lentil mixture into the pastry case.

5 Bake in a preheated oven, 200°C/400°F/Gas Mark 6, for 30 minutes until the filling is firm.

VARIATION
Add sweetcorn to the flan in step 3 for a colourful and tasty change.

Summer Fruit Salad

A mixture of soft summer fruits in an orange-flavoured syrup with a dash of port. Serve with low-fat yogurt.

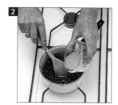

NUTRITIONAL INFORMATION

Calories 110	Sugars 26g	
Protein 1g	Fat 0.1g	
Carbohydrate . . .26g	Saturates 0g	

🍮 5 mins   🕐 10 mins

SERVES 6

I N G R E D I E N T S

6 tbsp caster sugar

5 tbsp water

grated rind and juice of 1 small orange

250 g/9 oz redcurrants, stripped from their stalks

2 tsp arrowroot

2 tbsp port

115 g/4 oz blackberries

115 g/4 oz blueberries

115 g/4 oz strawberries

225 g/8 oz raspberries

low-fat yogurt, to serve

1 Put the sugar, water and grated orange rind into a heavy-based saucepan and heat gently, stirring, until the sugar has completely dissolved.

COOK'S TIP

Although this salad is really best made with fresh fruits in season, you can achieve an acceptable result with frozen equivalents, with perhaps the exception of strawberries. You can buy frozen fruits of the forest, which would be ideal, in most supermarkets.

2 Add the redcurrants and orange juice, bring to the boil and simmer gently for 2–3 minutes.

3 Strain the fruit, reserving the syrup, and put into a bowl.

4 Blend the arrowroot with a little water. Return the syrup to the pan, add the arrowroot and bring to the boil, stirring constantly, until thickened.

5 Add the port and mix together well. Then pour the syrup over the redcurrants in the bowl.

6 Add the blackberries, blueberries, strawberries and raspberries. Mix the fruit together and set aside to cool until required. Serve in individual glass dishes with low-fat yogurt.

Chocolate Mousse

This is a light and fluffy mousse with a subtle hint of orange.
It is wickedly delicious served with a fresh fruit sauce.

NUTRITIONAL INFORMATION

Calories 164	Sugars 24g
Protein 5g	Fat 5g
Carbohydrate ...25g	Saturates 3g

 2¼ hrs   5 mins

SERVES 8

I N G R E D I E N T S

100 g/3½ oz plain chocolate, melted

300 ml/10 fl oz natural yogurt

150 ml/5 fl oz Quark

4 tbsp caster sugar

1 tbsp orange juice

1 tbsp brandy

1½ tsp gelatine, or gelozone
   (vegetarian gelatine)

135 ml/4½ fl oz cold water

2 large egg whites

TO DECORATE

dark and white chocolate, roughly grated

orange rind

1 Put the melted chocolate, yogurt, Quark, sugar, orange juice and brandy in a food processor or blender and process for 30 seconds. Transfer the mixture to a large bowl.

2 Sprinkle the gelatine or gelozone over the water and stir until dissolved.

3 Put the gelatine or gelozone and water in a saucepan and bring to the boil for 2 minutes. Cool slightly, then thoroughly stir into the chocolate mixture.

4 Whisk the egg whites until stiff peaks form and fold into the chocolate mixture using a metal spoon.

5 Line a 500-g/1 lb 2-oz loaf tin with clingfilm. Spoon the mousse into the pan. Chill in the refrigerator for about 2 hours until set. Turn the mousse out onto a serving plate, decorate with grated chocolate and orange rind and serve.

COOK'S TIP

For a quick fruit sauce, process a can of mandarin segments in natural juice in a food processor and press through a sieve. Stir in 1 tablespoon honey and serve with the mousse.

Ricotta-lemon Cheesecake

Italian bakers pride themselves on their baked ricotta cheesecakes, studded with fruit soaked in spirits.

NUTRITIONAL INFORMATION

Calories 188   Sugars 21g
Protein . . . . .6g   Fat 8g
Carbohydrate . . .23g   Saturates 4g

3¾ hrs   30–40 mins

SERVES 6–8

INGREDIENTS

55 g/2 oz sultanas

3 tbsp Marsala or grappa

butter, for greasing

2 tbsp semolina, plus extra for dusting

350 g/12 oz ricotta cheese, drained

3 large egg yolks, beaten

100 g/3½ oz caster sugar

3 tbsp lemon juice

2 tbsp crystallised orange peel,
    finely chopped

rind of 2 large lemons, finely grated

TO DECORATE

icing sugar

sprigs of fresh mint

redcurrants or berries (optional)

1 Soak the sultanas in the Marsala or grappa in a small bowl for about 30 minutes or until the liquid has been absorbed and the fruit is swollen.

2 Cut out a circle of baking paper to fit the bottom of a loose-based 20-cm/ 8-inch round cake tin that is about 5 cm/2 inches deep. Grease the sides and base of the tin and line the base. Dust with semolina and tip out the excess.

3 Using a wooden spoon, press the ricotta cheese though a nylon sieve into a bowl. Beat in the egg yolks, sugar, semolina and lemon juice and continue beating until blended.

4 Fold in the sultanas, orange peel and lemon rind. Pour into the prepared tin and smooth the surface.

5 Bake the cheesecake in the centre of a preheated oven, 180°C/350°F/Gas Mark 4, for 30–40 minutes until firm when you press the top and coming away slightly from the sides of the tin.

6 Turn off the oven and open the door. Leave the cheesecake to cool in the switched-off oven for 2–3 hours. To serve, remove from the tin and transfer to a plate. Sift over a layer of icing sugar from at least 30 cm/12 inches above the cheesecake to dust the top and sides lightly. Decorate with mint, and redcurrants or berries if using.

Practical
Low-fat Dishes

p^3

This is a P3 Book
First published in 2002

P3
Queen Street House
4 Queen Street
Bath BA1 1HE, UK

Copyright © Parragon 2002

ISBN: 0-75259-039-1

Printed in China

NOTE

This book uses metric and imperial measurements. Follow the same units
of measurement throughout; do not mix metric and imperial.
All spoon measurements are level: teaspoons are assumed to be 5 ml, and
tablespoons are assumed to be 15 ml. Unless otherwise stated,
milk is assumed to be full fat, eggs and individual vegetables such as potatoes
are medium, and pepper is freshly ground black pepper.

The nutritional information provided for each recipe is per serving or per person.
Optional ingredients, variations or serving suggestions have
not been included in the calculations. The times given for each recipe are an approximate
guide only because the preparation times may differ according to the techniques used by
different people and the cooking times may vary as a result of the type of oven used.

Recipes using raw or very lightly cooked eggs should be
avoided by children, the elderly, pregnant women, convalescents,
and anyone suffering from an illness.